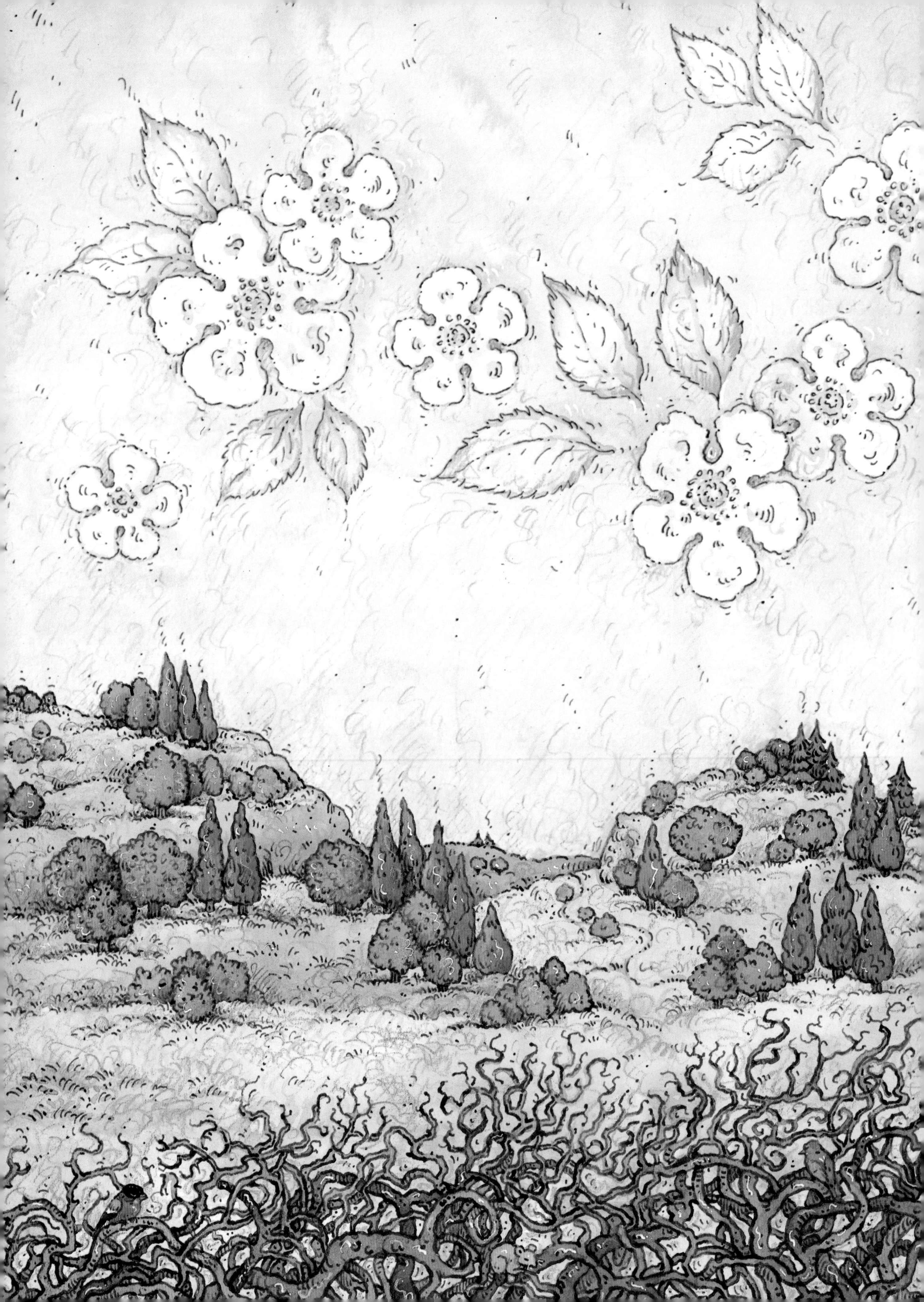

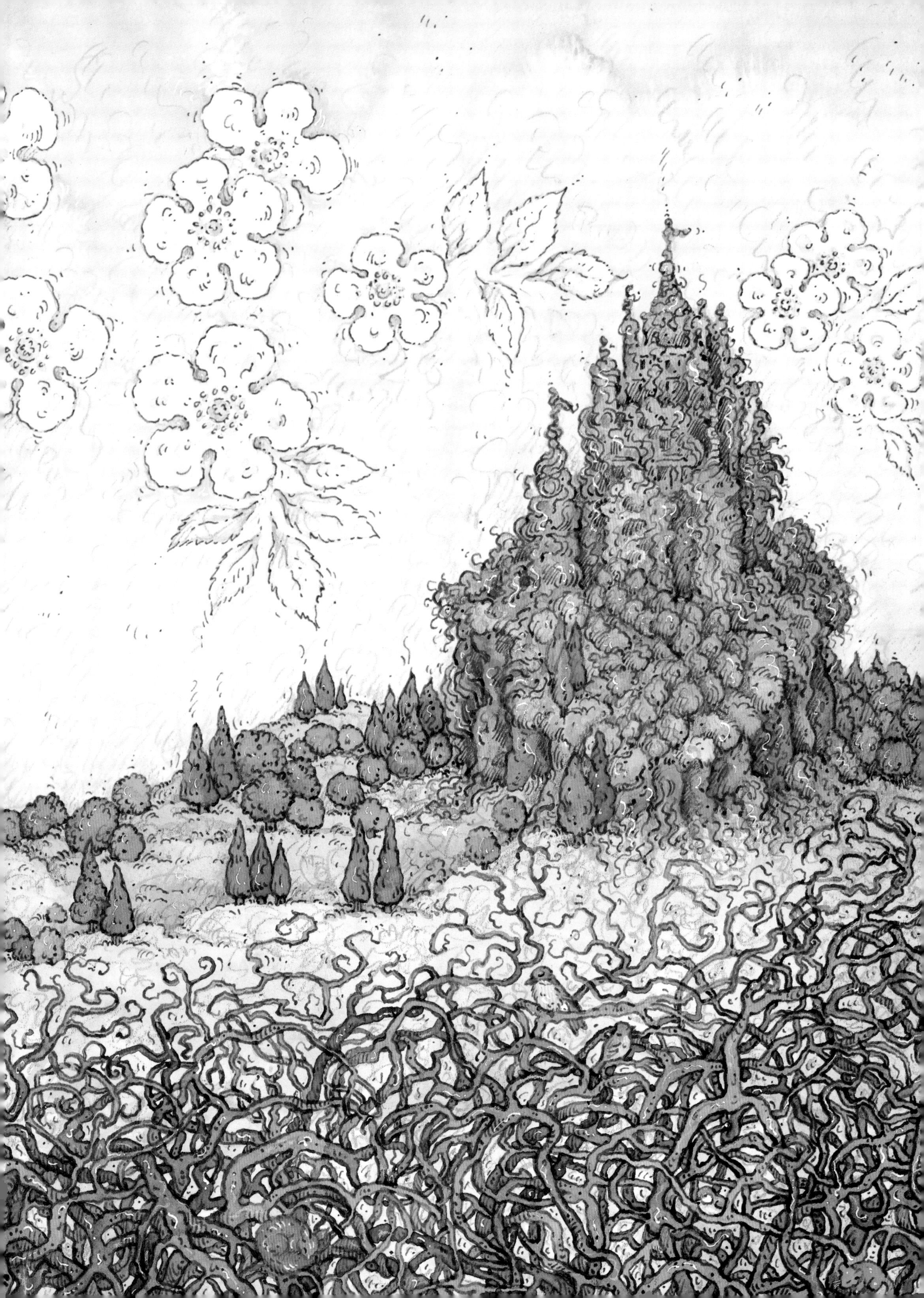

Copyright © 1995 by Nord-Süd Verlag AG, Gossau Zürich, Switzerland
First published in Switzerland under the title Dornröschen
English translation copyright © 1995 by North-South Books Inc.

First published in the United States, Great Britain, Canada,
Australia, and New Zealand in 1995 by North-South Books,
an imprint of Nord-Süd Verlag AG, Gossau Zürich, Switzerland.

Distributed in the United States by North-South Books Inc., New York.

Library of Congress Cataloging-in-Publication Data is available.
A CIP catalogue record for this book is available from The British Library.
ISBN 1-55858-399-8 (TRADE BINDING)
ISBN 1-55858-400-5 (LIBRARY BINDING)

1 3 5 7 9 TB 10 8 6 4 2
1 3 5 7 9 LB 10 8 6 4 2
Printed in Belgium

The Sleeping Beauty

A Fairy Tale by Jacob & Wilhelm Grimm

Illustrated by Monika Laimgruber

TRANSLATED BY ANTHEA BELL

North-South Books

NEW YORK · LONDON

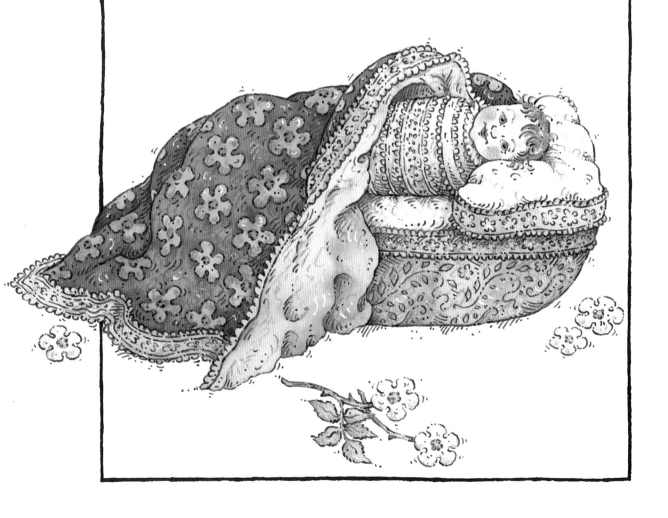

Once upon a time there lived a king and queen who had no children. Every day they said to each other, "Oh, if only we could have a child!" But they never did.

Now one day, while the queen was bathing, a frog hopped up out of the water and told her, "Your wish will be granted. You will have a daughter before the year is over."

It turned out just as the frog had said. The queen had a baby, such a beautiful little girl that the king was beside himself with joy. He decided to hold a great banquet. As well as inviting his family, friends, and acquaintances, he asked the wise women of his kingdom to come and wish the child well.

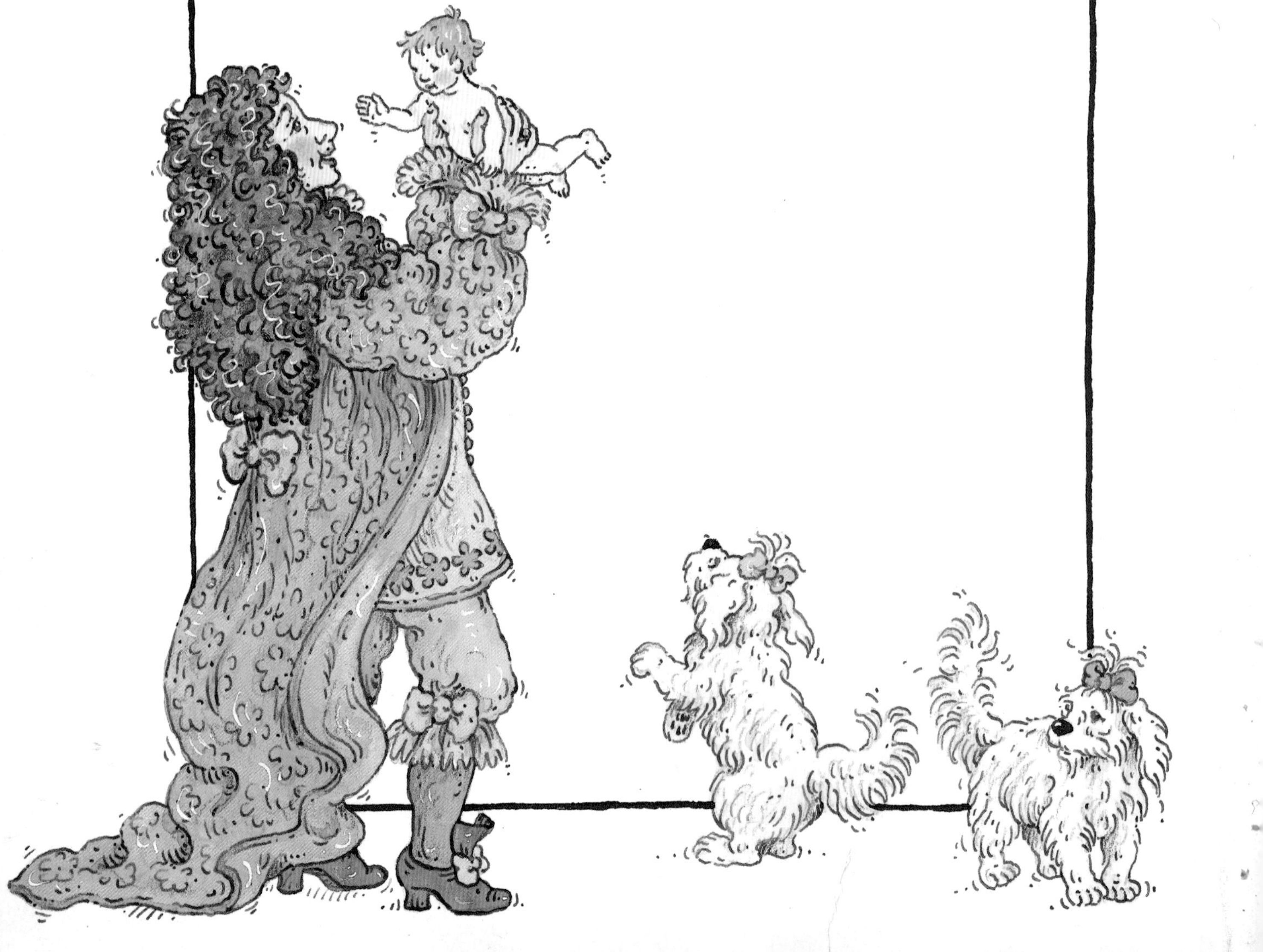

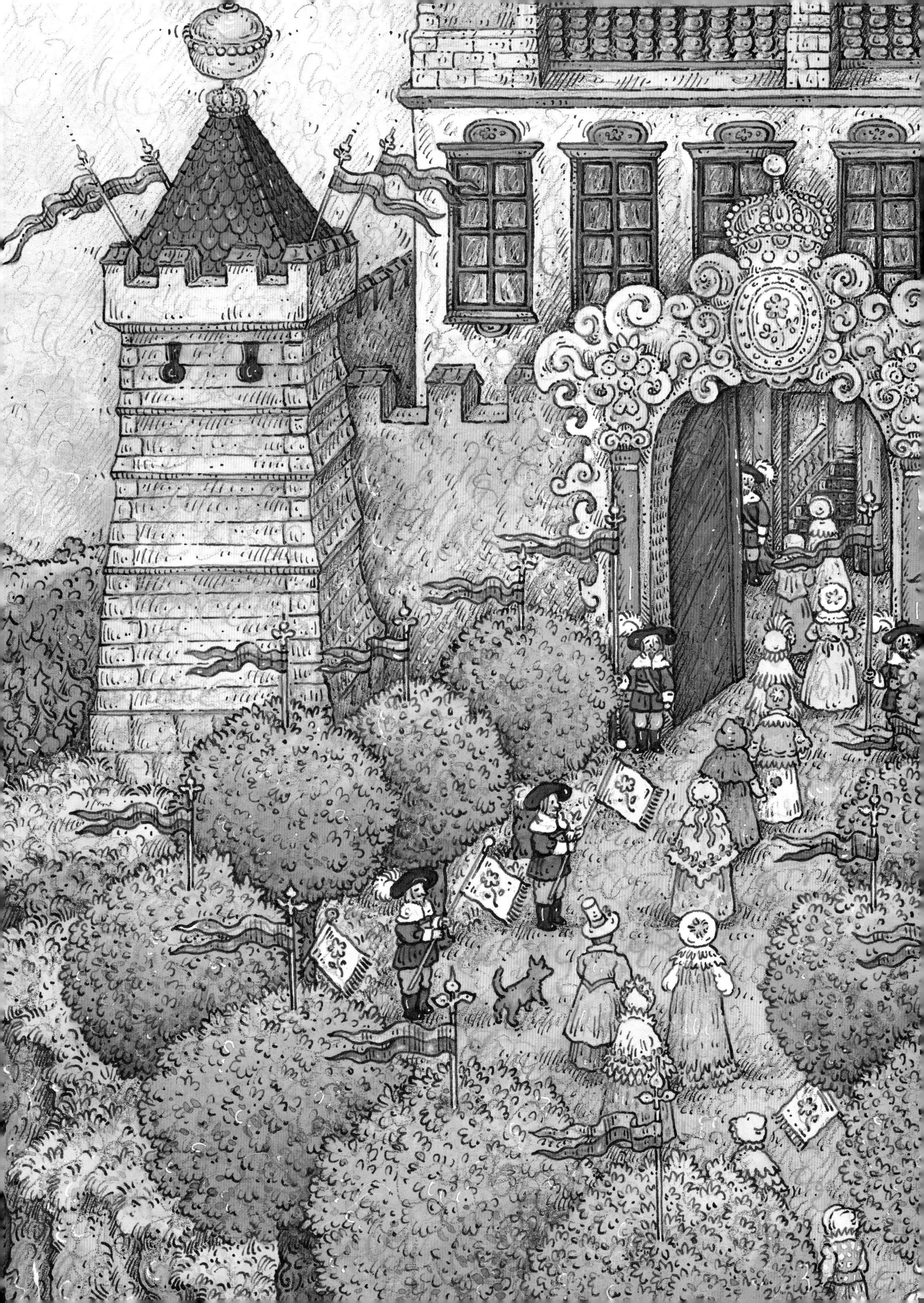

There were thirteen wise women and they were to eat from golden plates, but as there were only twelve plates, one was not invited.

The banquet was held, and it was splendid. When it was over, the wise women gave the baby their magic gifts. One gave her goodness, another beauty, a third wealth, and so on, until she had everything in the world you could wish for.

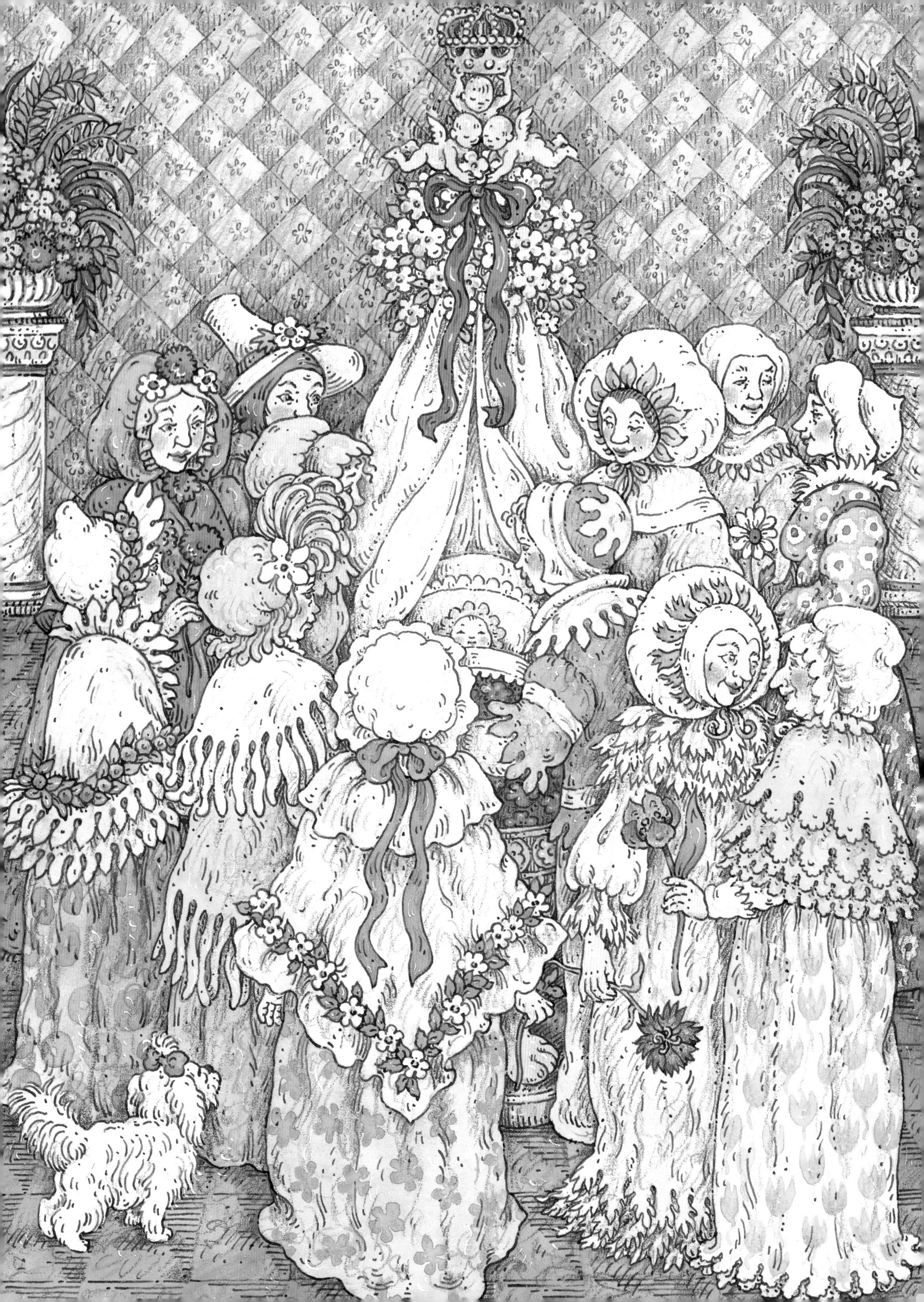

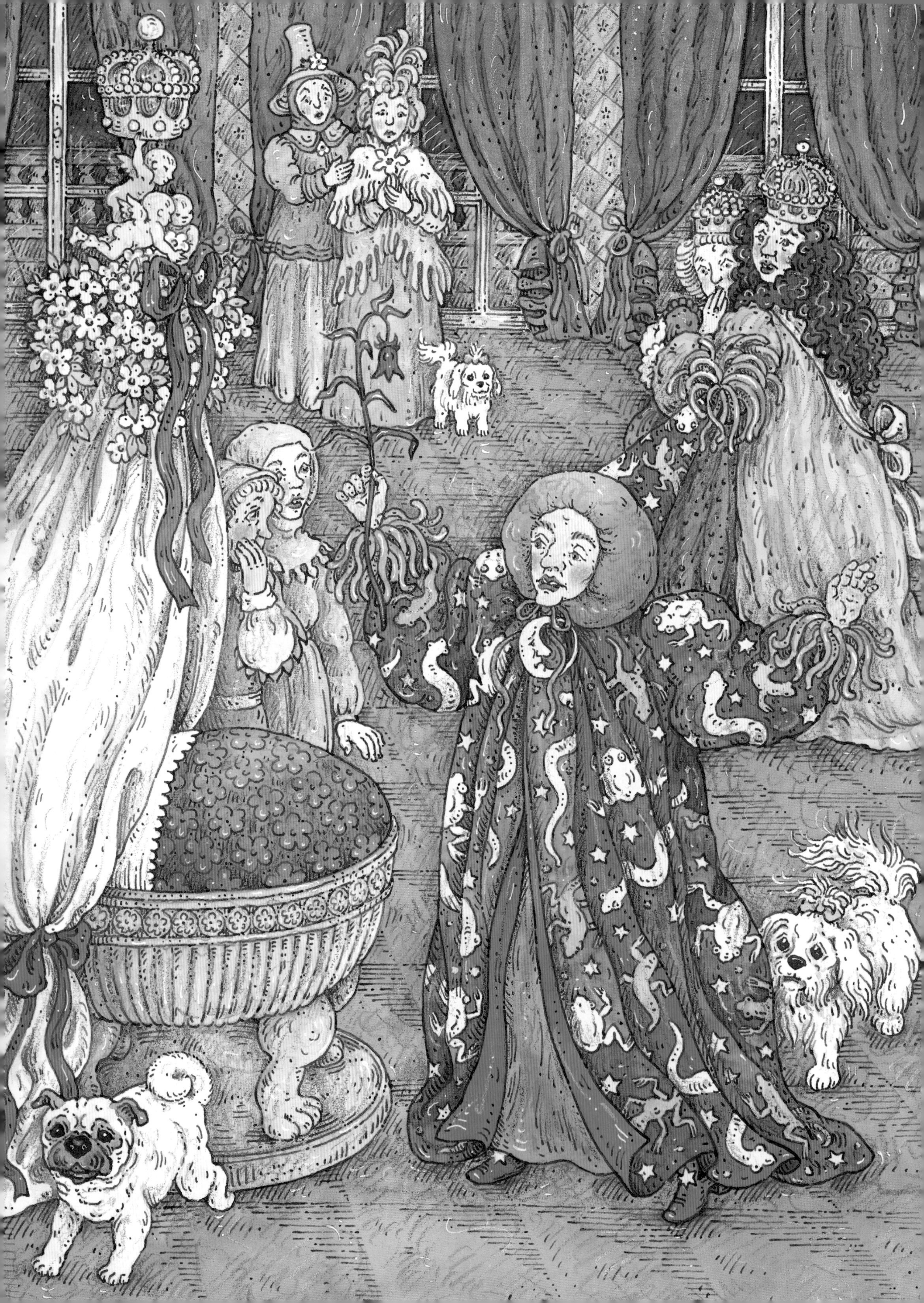

When eleven of the wise women had given their gifts, the thirteenth suddenly walked in. She wanted her revenge for not being invited, and without greeting or even looking at anyone, she said in a loud voice, "When the king's daughter is fifteen, she will prick her finger on a spindle and fall down dead." Then, without another word, she turned and left the banquet hall.

As the guests stood there, horrified, out stepped the twelfth wise woman, who had not yet given her gift. She could not break the wicked spell but only soften it, so she said, "The king's daughter will not die but fall fast asleep, and she will sleep for a hundred years."

hoping to keep his daughter from such a fate, the king ordered all the spindles in his kingdom to be burnt.

As for the little girl herself, all the wishes the wise women had made for her came true. She was so beautiful, good, kind, and clever that everyone who set eyes on her loved her.

It so happened that on the very day of her fifteenth birthday the king and queen were not at home, and the princess was alone in the castle. She explored the whole place, going from room to room just as she liked until at last she came to an old tower. She climbed the narrow spiral staircase and found a little door.

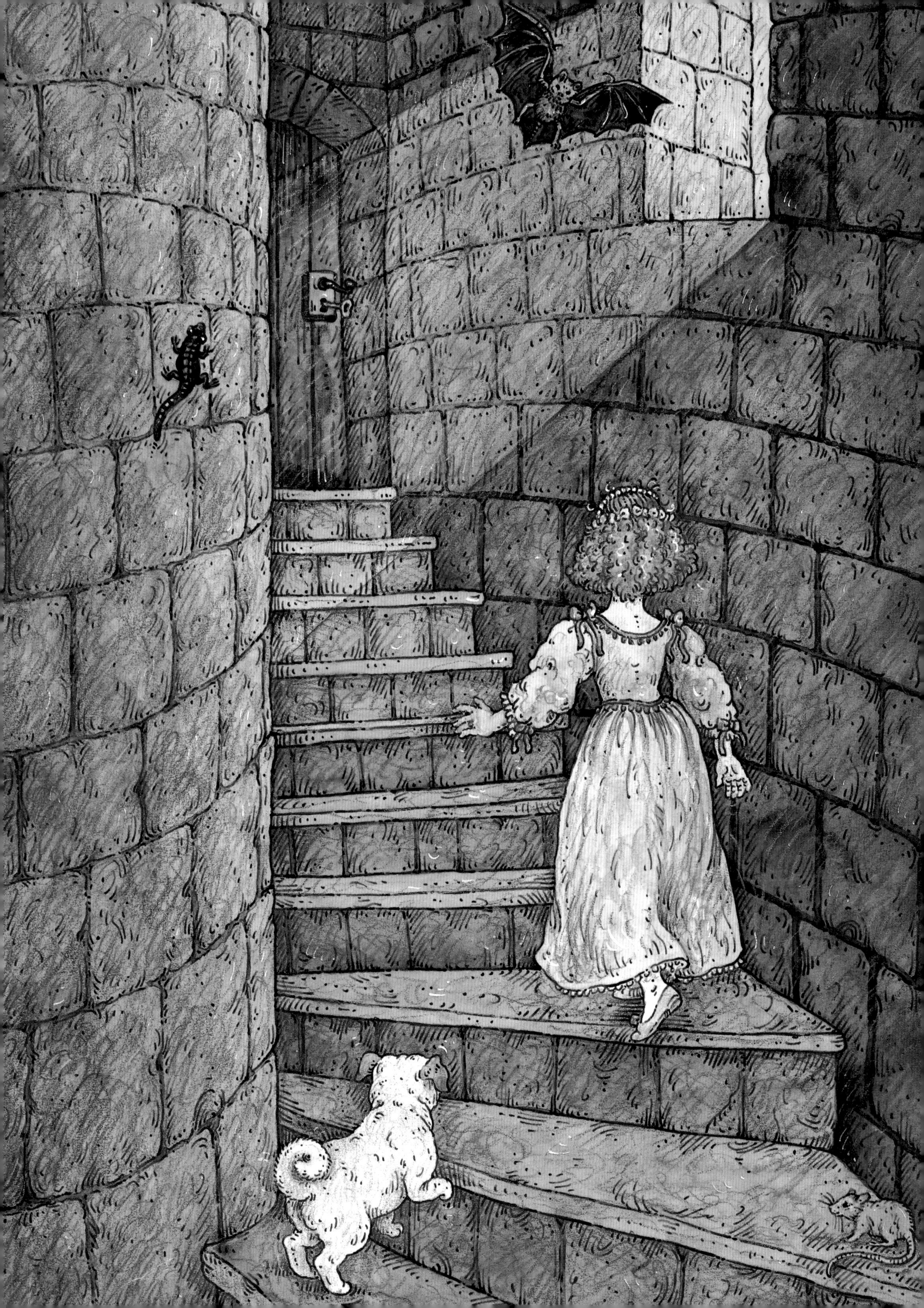

There was a rusty key in the lock, and when she turned it, the door opened. She saw a small room, and an old woman sitting inside it with a spindle, busy spinning flax.

"Good day," said the princess. "What are you doing?"

"I'm spinning," said the old woman, nodding her head.

"What's that jumping about?" asked the girl. She took the spindle to try spinning a thread herself, but no sooner had she touched it than the magic spell came true and she pricked her finger. The moment she felt it, she fell on the bed in the room and a deep sleep came over her.

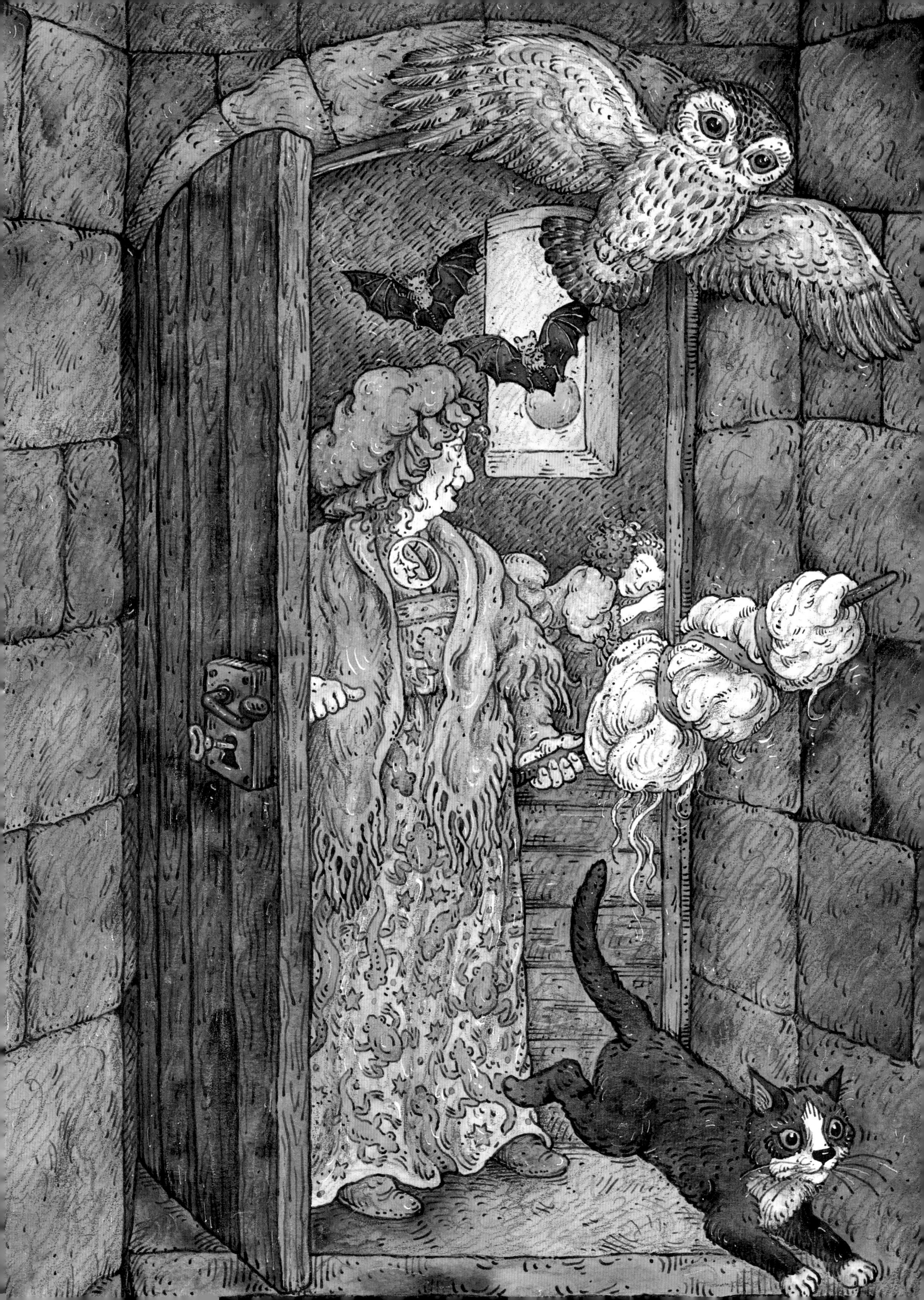

The same deep sleep overcame the whole castle: the king and queen, who had just come home and entered the great hall, fell asleep, and the entire court with them. The horses slept in the stables, the dogs in the yard, the doves on the roof, the flies on the wall, even the fire flickering on the hearth burned low and slept, while the meat roasting on the spit stopped crackling, and the cook, who had been about to box the kitchen boy's ears, fell asleep with his hand in the air. Then the wind itself died down, and not a leaf stirred on the trees outside the castle.

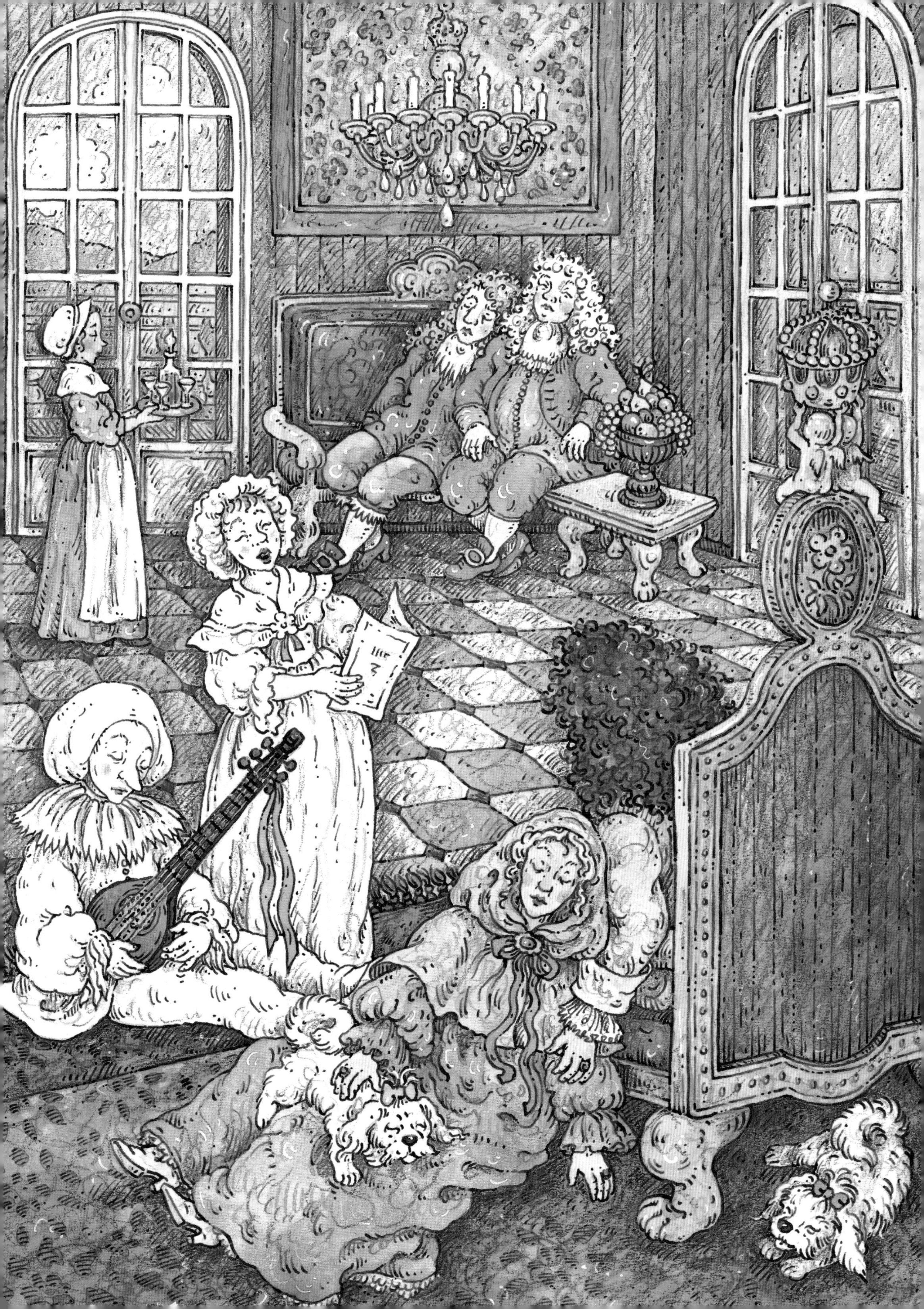

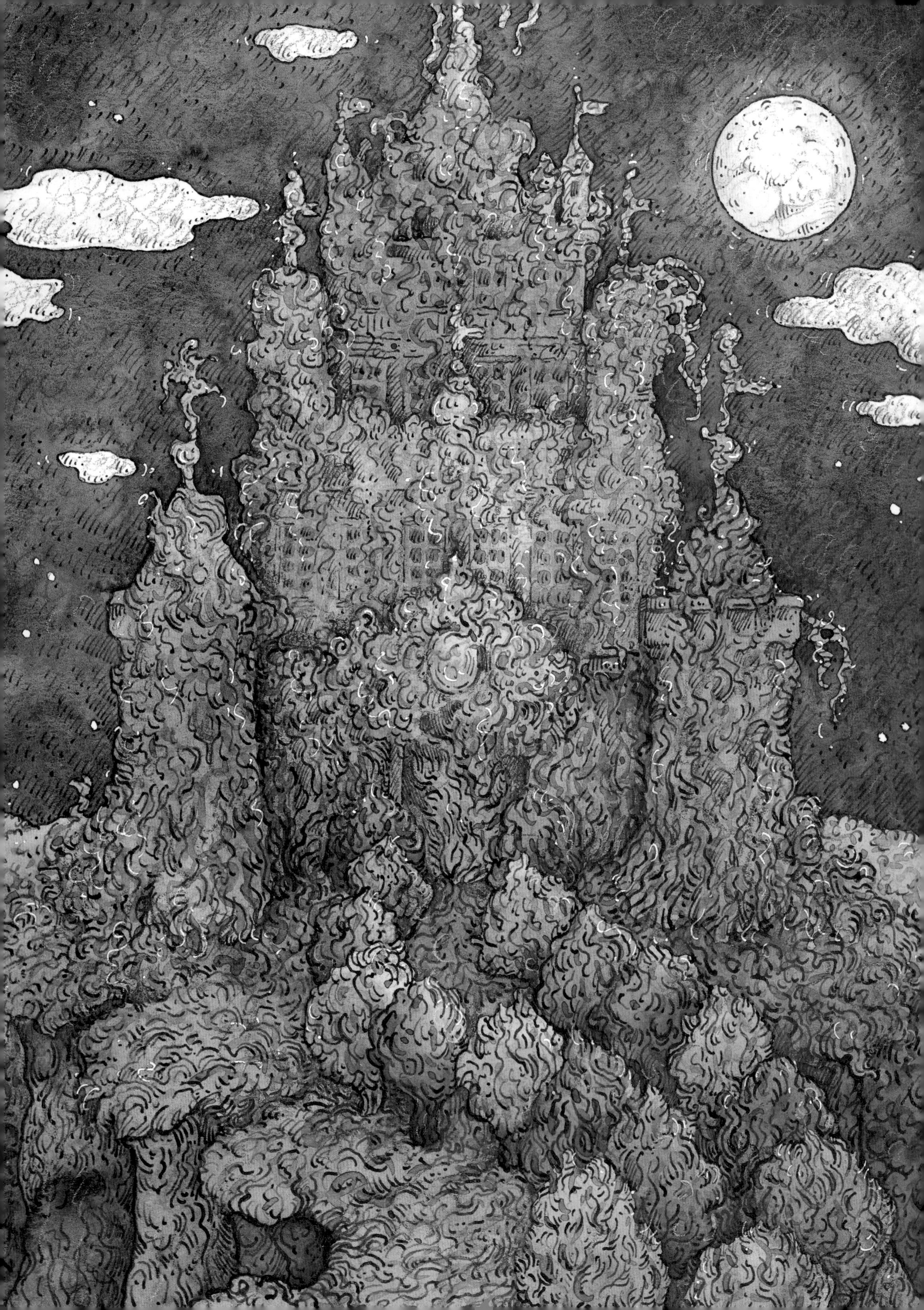

Soon a thorny hedge began to grow around the castle. It grew higher and higher every year, until at last it surrounded the whole castle, towering above it so that there was nothing to be seen, not even the flag on the rooftop.

As the years passed, the country folk told tales of the lovely Sleeping Beauty, for that was what they called the king's daughter. From time to time princes came and tried to get through the hedge into the castle beyond. But they never could, for the thorns clung fast together, as if they had hands. When the young men were caught up in them, they could not get free again, and died a miserable death.

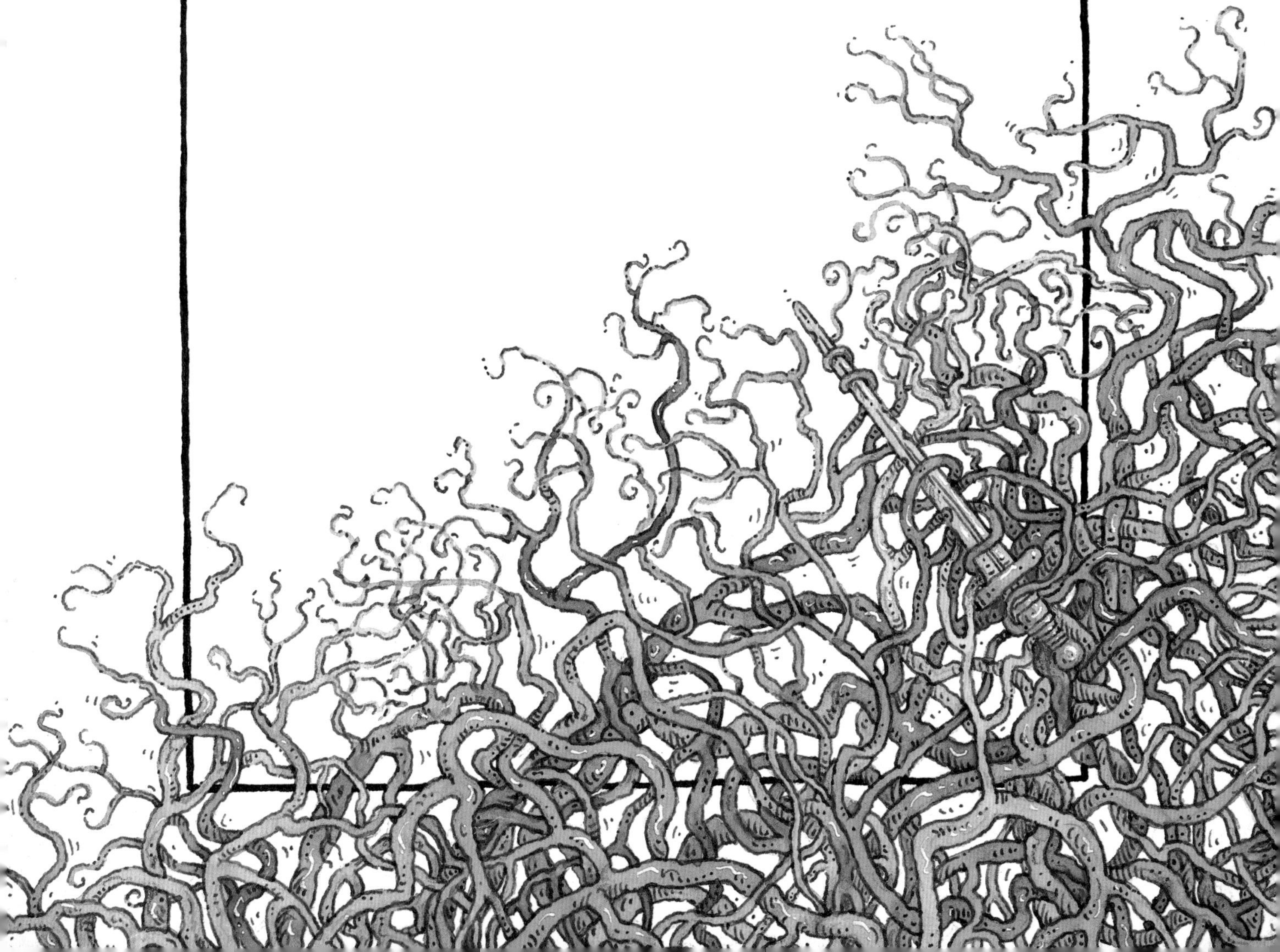

After many long years, yet another prince came to that country, and met an old man who told him about the thorny hedge and the castle said to lie beyond it. A lovely princess called Sleeping Beauty had been asleep there for a hundred years, said the old man, and all the princes who tried to break through the hedge were caught in the thorns and died miserably.

"I am not afraid," said the prince. "I will go there and see the lovely Sleeping Beauty." And however much the old man advised him against it, he would not listen.

But it so happened that the hundred years were over, and the day had come for Sleeping Beauty to wake up. When the prince reached the hedge, it was covered with big, beautiful flowers instead of thorns, and it opened of its own accord to let him through unharmed, closing into a hedge behind him.

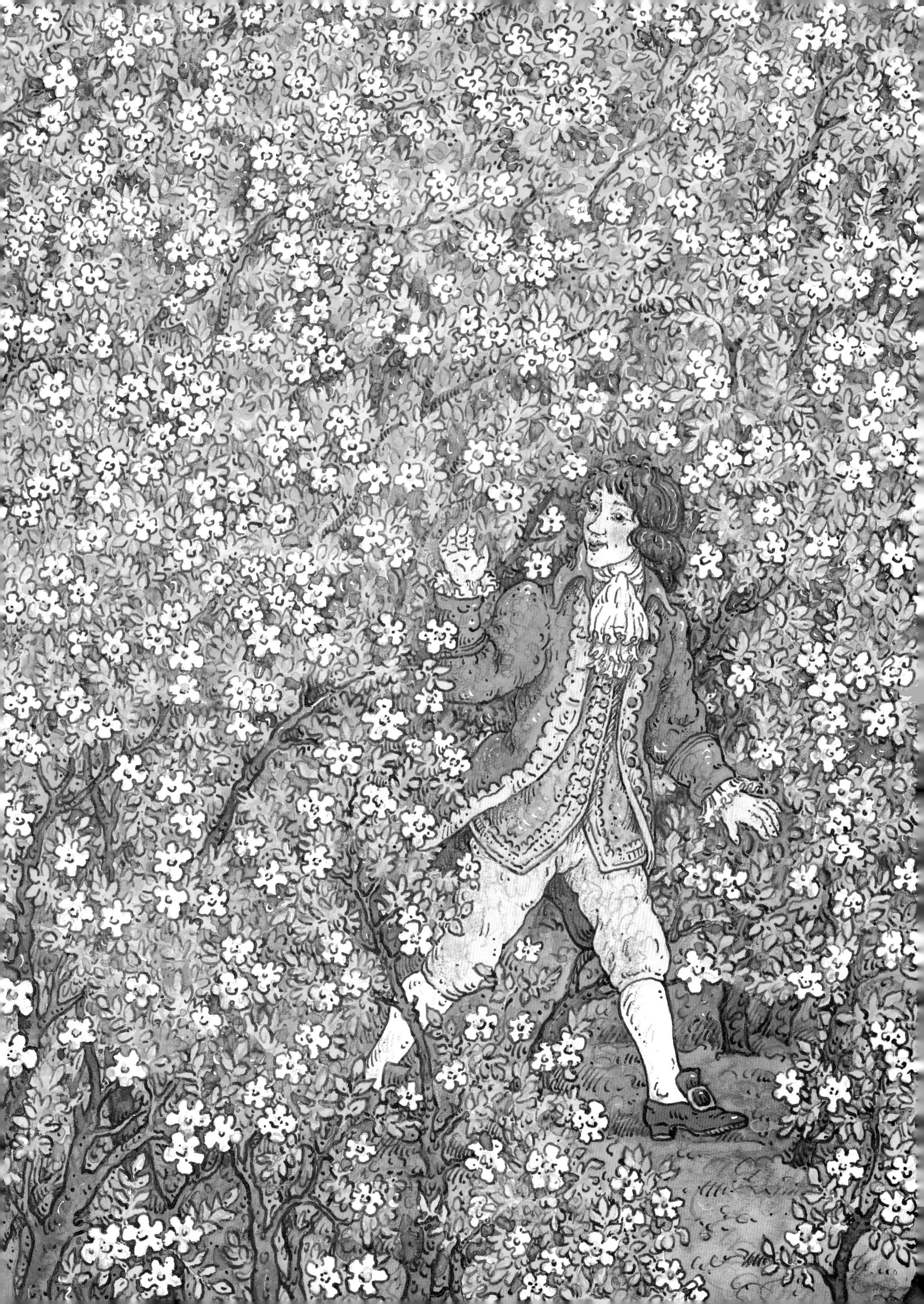

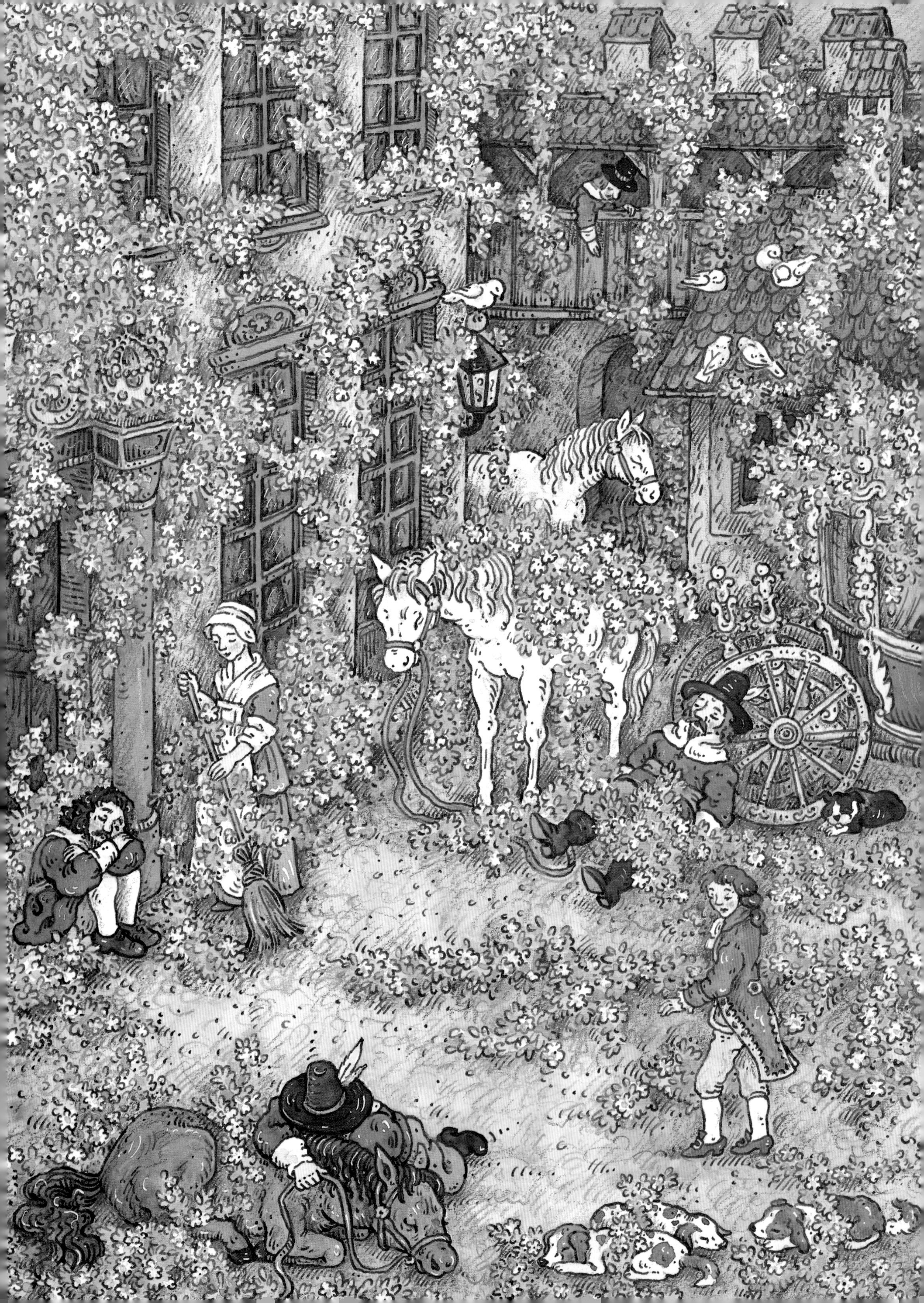

In the castle courtyard, he saw the horses and the spotted hounds lying asleep, and the doves sitting on the roof with their heads tucked under their wings.

When he entered the castle, the flies were asleep on the wall, the cook in the kitchen still had his hand raised to hit the kitchen boy, and the maidservant was sitting with a black chicken ready for plucking. The prince went on, and saw the whole court lying asleep in the great hall, with the king and queen by the throne. He went further on, and it was all so still he could hear his own breath. At last he came to the tower and opened the door into the little room where Sleeping Beauty lay.

She was so beautiful that the prince could not take his eyes off her. He bent down and gave her a kiss.

As soon as he kissed her, Sleeping Beauty opened her eyes, woke up, and gazed lovingly at him.

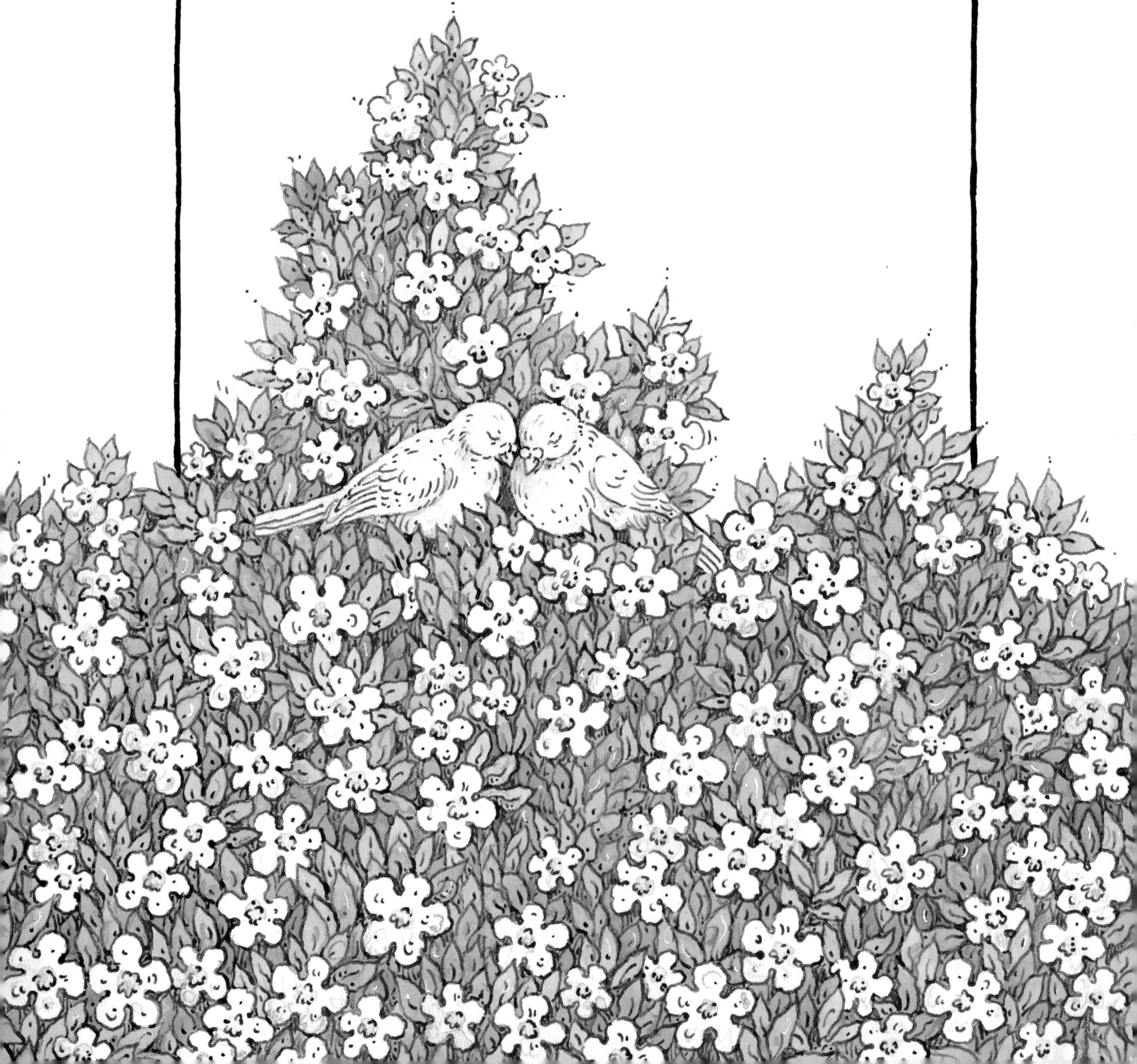

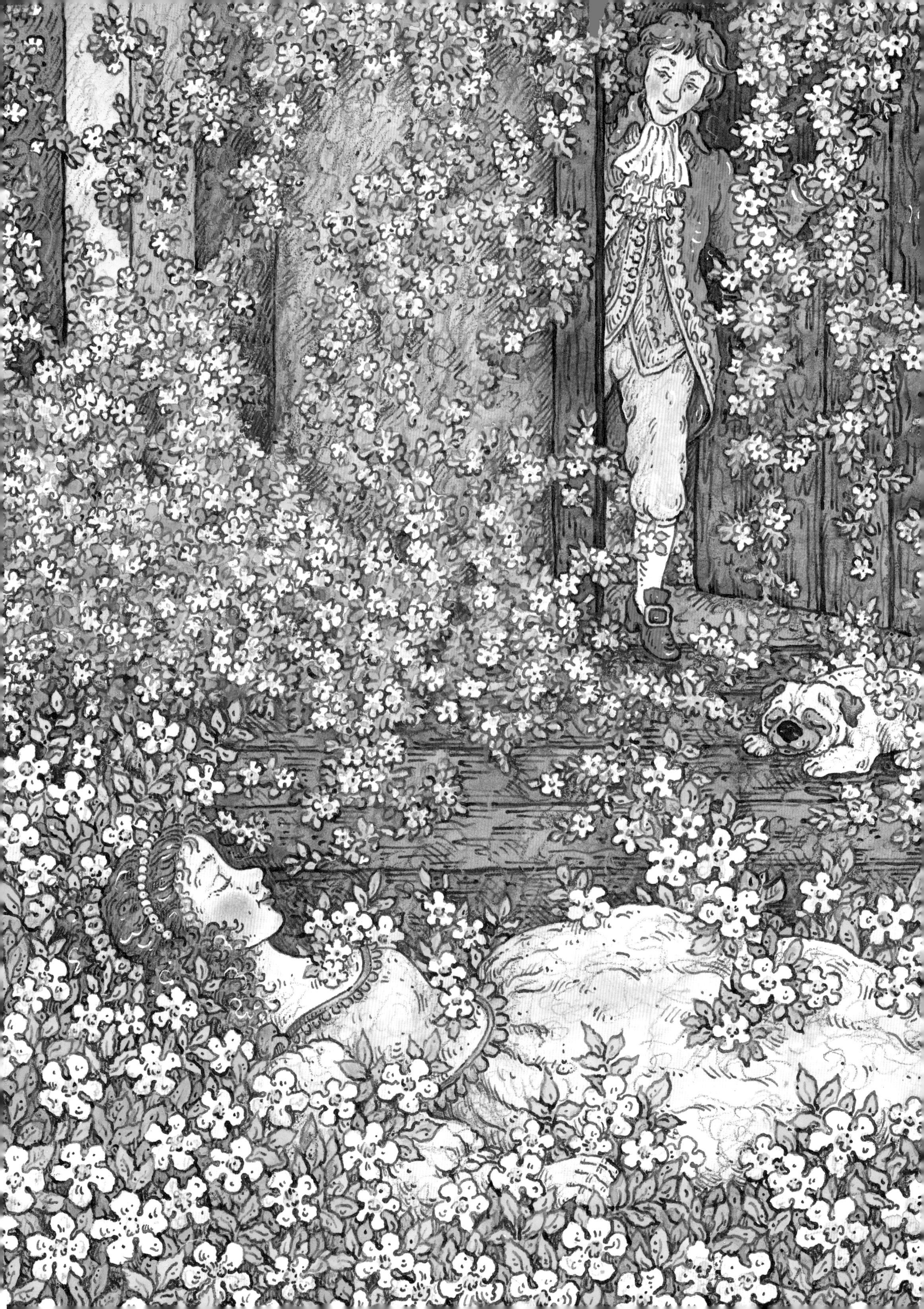

They went down the stairs together. The king and queen woke up, and so did the court, all staring at one another wide-eyed. And the horses out in the yard stood up and shook themselves; the hounds leaped up, wagging their tails; the doves on the roof took their heads out from under their wings, looked around, and flew away; the flies went on crawling up the walls; the fire on the kitchen hearth flared up, the meat roasting on the spit began to crackle again; the cook boxed the kitchen boy's ears so hard that he screeched; and the maidservant went on plucking the chicken.

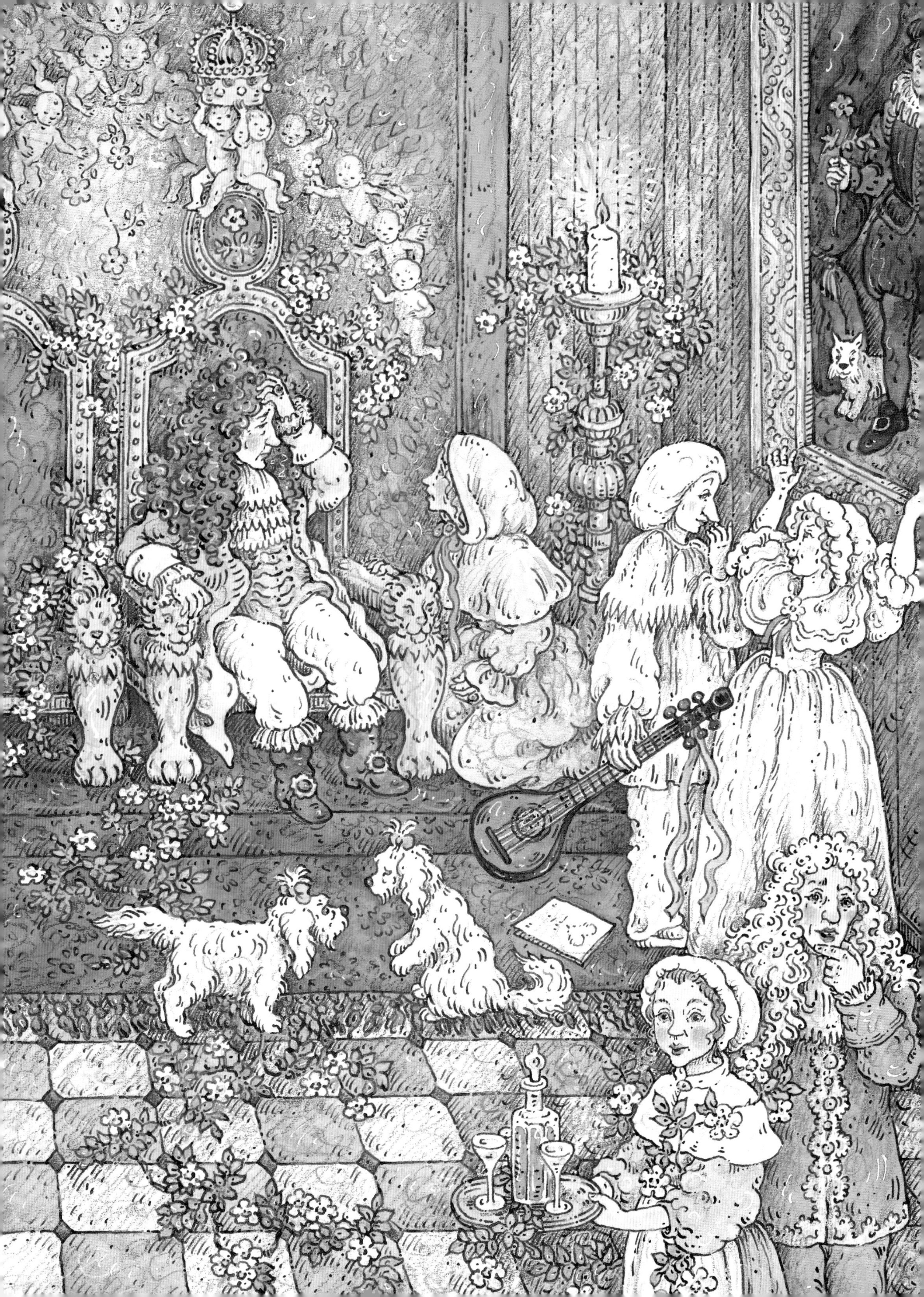

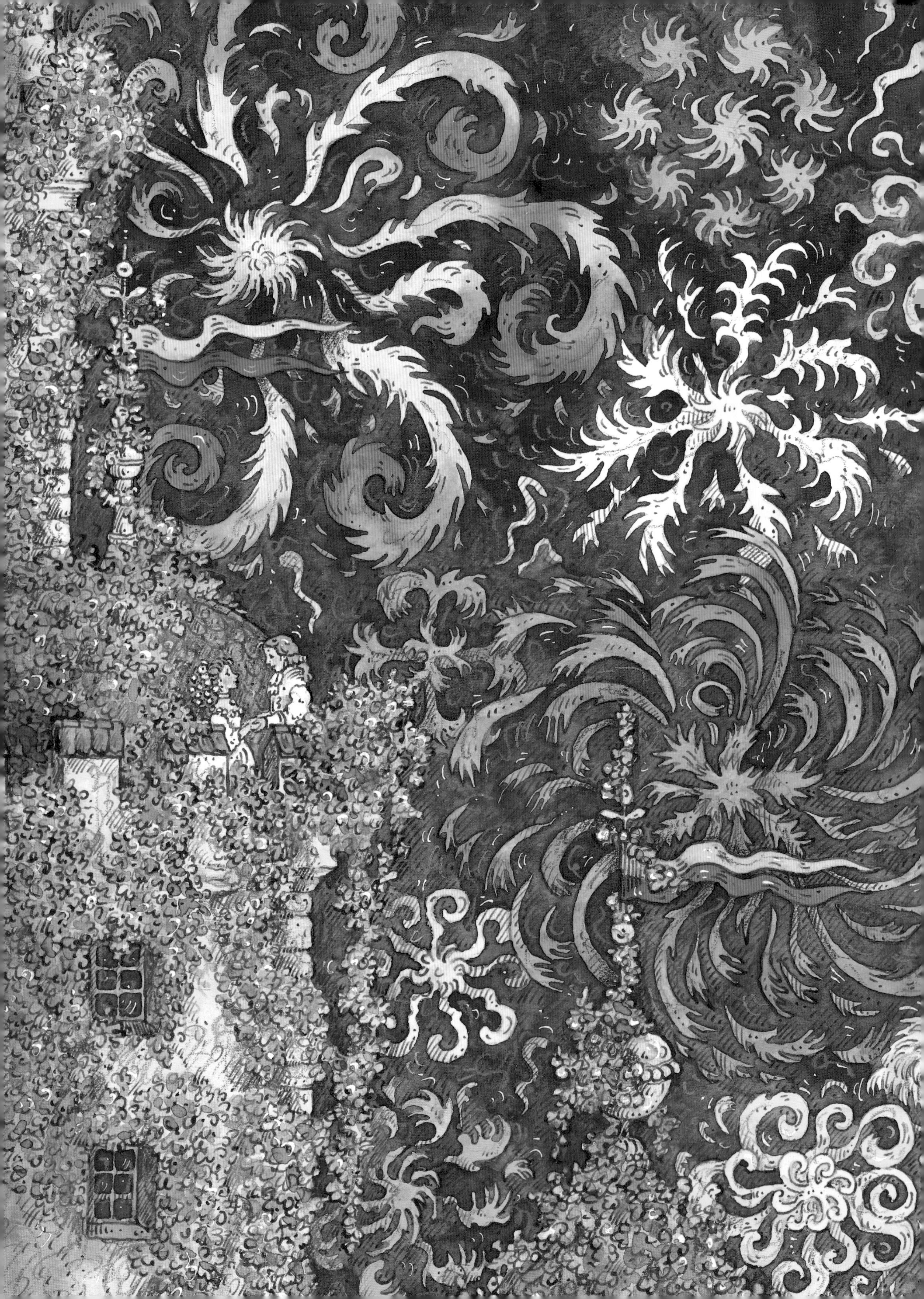

Then the wedding of the prince and Sleeping Beauty was celebrated with great magnificence, and they lived happily ever after until the end of their days.

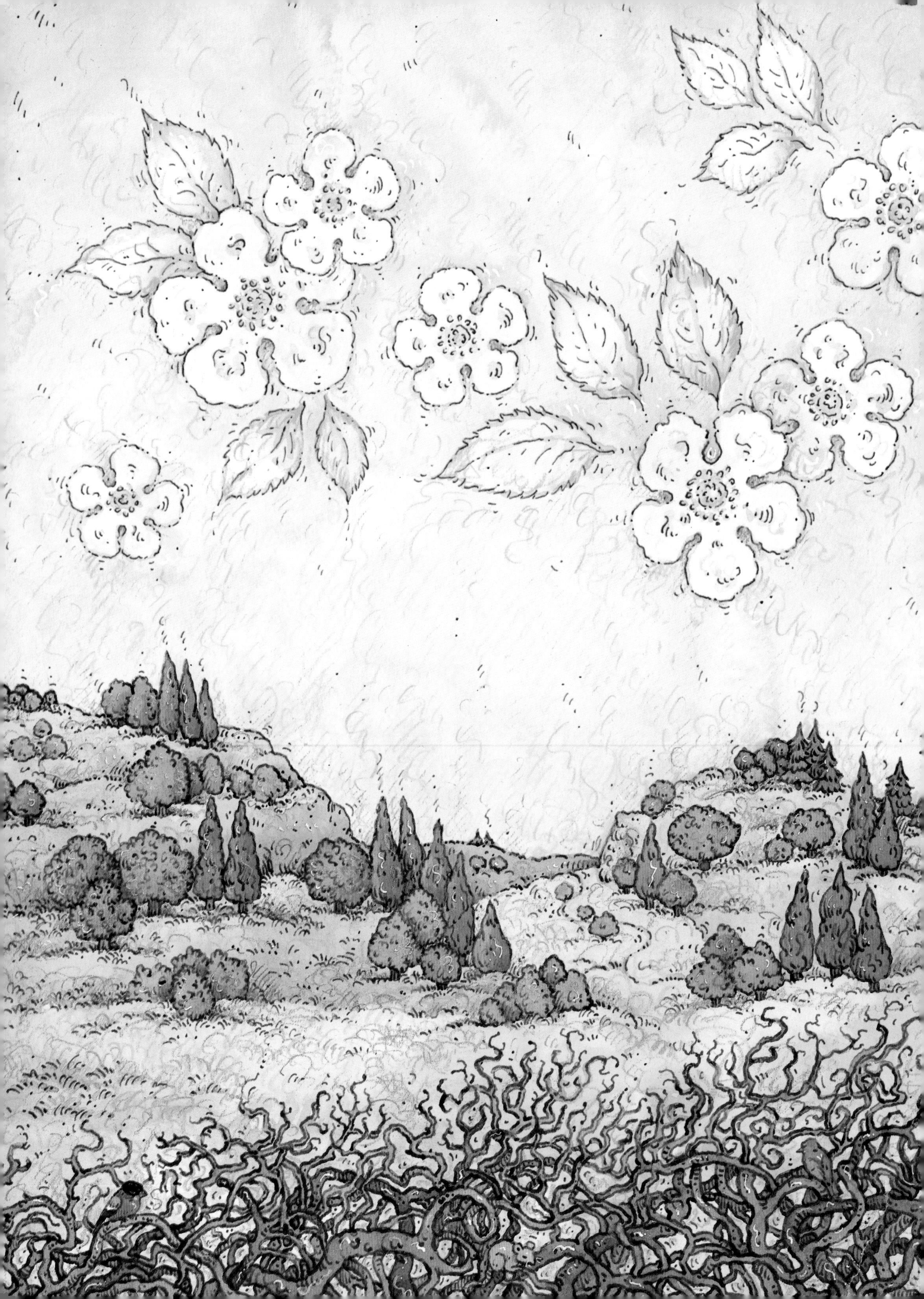

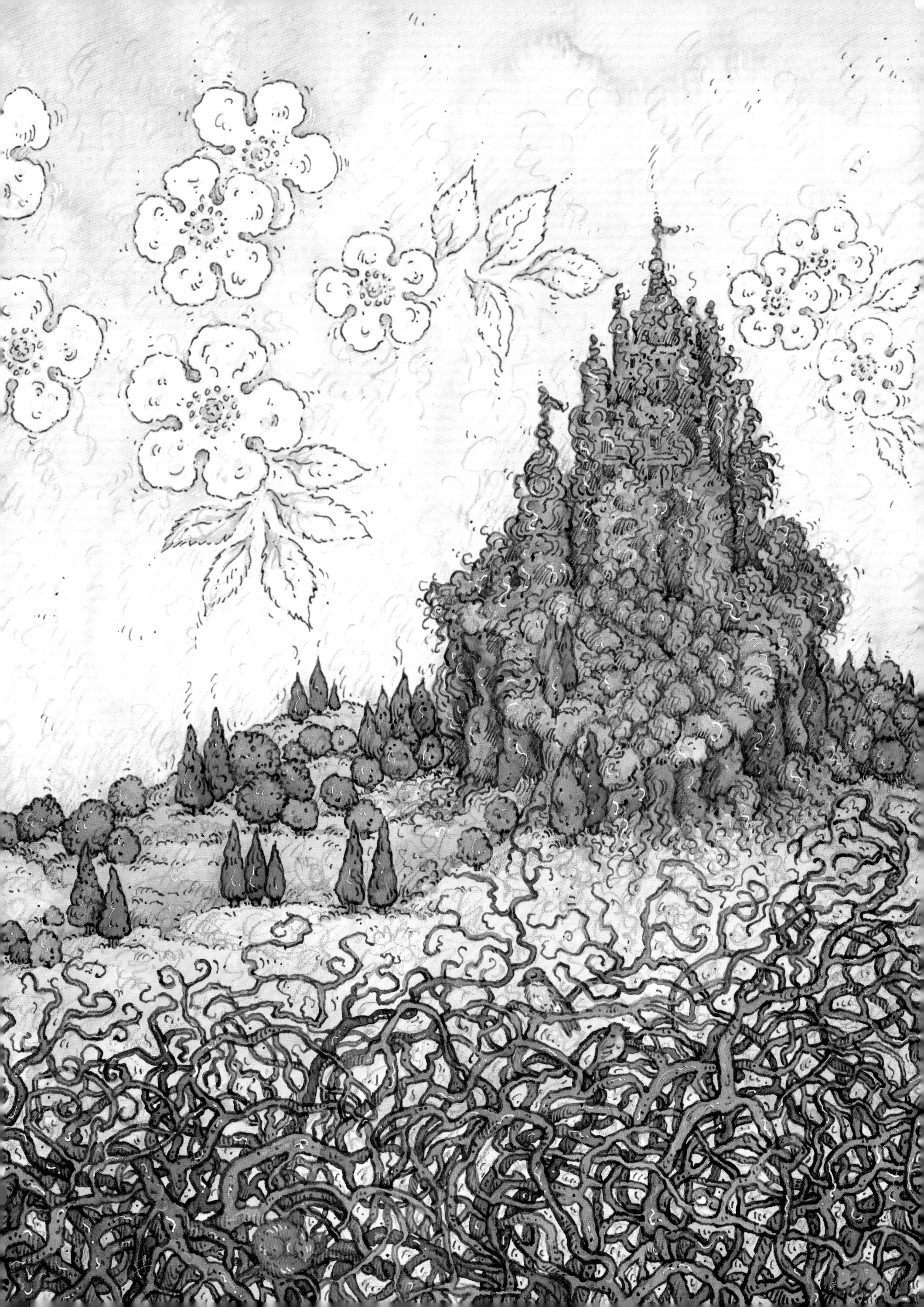